The three guys were talking to each other real loud, as though they meant us to hear them. Then one of them reached out and grabbed me by my sweater sleeve. He pulled me up to him and put his face against mine. Then he spit. The spit stuck on my cheek. It felt thick and warm.

"Whattaya know," he said. "A nigger lover. That's what you are, right, punk? A nigger lover."

The other two guys had pulled Peter away. I saw one of them push his knee into Peter's stomach and knock him down. The other guy rolled Peter over and twisted his arms behind his back.

"This town don't want people like you," one of the guys said to Peter in a low voice. "You *or* your brother."

Other Bullseye Books you will enjoy

The Secret Life of the Underwear Champ
  by Betty Miles
The Kid in the Red Jacket by Barbara Park
Skinnybones by Barbara Park
There's a Boy in the Girls' Bathroom
  by Louis Sachar

All It Takes Is Practice

Betty Miles

Bullseye Books • Alfred A. Knopf
New York

DR. M. JERRY WEISS, Distinguished Service Professor of Communications at Jersey City State College, is the educational consultant for Bullseye Books. A past chair of the International Reading Association President's Advisory Committee on Intellectual Freedom, he travels frequently to give workshops on the use of trade books in schools.

For David

1

The good thing about basketball is you can practice it alone.

I don't usually ask anybody over after school to practice with me. It's not that I don't want to. It's just that it gets to be such a big deal, asking different kids till you find somebody who doesn't say "I don't know" or "Maybe" or just plain "No." Once in a while, I ask this guy in my class, Robert, but he usually has something else to do.

Coach Schultz says I have the speed to make a good player. The thing is, he doesn't know how much better I play at home. Neither do the other kids. In school we have boys' basketball with the other fifth grade, so there are always lots of kids watching when you go for a jump shot or a free throw. I get nervous when a lot of people watch me. My plan is to keep practicing at home till I get so good and sure of myself I can play in front of anyone. Someday I'll surprise them. My ambition is to be a point guard with the New York Knicks.

I wish a basketball scout, or even some kid, would happen to come along Seneca Street when I'm really sinking them in. I once thought of writing a letter to the junior-high coach: "A tip. Check out the kid who practices by himself every day at 125 Seneca. He's small, but he's smooth and dedicated." I could sign it "A Sports Fan." But what if they found out it was my handwriting?

Too bad Alison Henning's not a basketball scout. She's about the only person who knows how good I am. Alison's in my class and she lives on my street. We walk home together and sometimes she comes over to watch me practice. Sometimes I let her shoot a few. She's pretty good, better than lots of the guys in our gym class. She wants to be on the girls' team in junior high. I bet she could, only she doesn't have any regular place to practice. The girls don't get basketball in gym in our school.

Every time I work out I try to practice something new, like shooting lefty. (I'm right-handed.) It's interesting to train yourself to do something new like that. I bet I could even learn to write left-handed if I worked at it. It just takes practice. I know you can't change some things, like how tall you are or if you're retarded or something. But every time I shoot lefty, it gets easier.

Sometimes I wonder if you could train yourself not to be shy, just by practice. But that kind of thing is probably harder to learn. Still, I'm thinking about trying it. My parents say that to make friends you just have to act friendly, and people will act friendly back. Well, I do that some, and it works okay. I mean, nobody *hates* me or anything. But I don't have a really best friend, the kind you don't have to plan what you're going to say to ahead of time.

It would be neat if the new kid who came to school today turned out to be my friend. His name is Peter Baker. Miss Hansen asked me to show him around school. He acted friendly, but this was just his first day. You can't tell with new kids.

I dribbled up my driveway, thinking about school and the new kid. I wished he could see me now. I stopped, pivoted, ran up, and dropped one right in, lefty. When I get going, I'm really hot.

This Peter moved here from someplace near New York City. He never really lived *in* the city, but he's been there. He went to a Knicks game once, but they lost. He also went to the Empire State Building. He said it makes your ears pop to go up in the elevator. He wasn't showing off about the Knicks or the Empire State Building. I asked him. Especially about the Knicks. He seemed to like telling me things. And he sort of hung out with me all day, because he was new.

At the end of the day, Peter piled his books in front of him on the table and just sat there, waiting. I guess he expected Miss Hansen to dismiss us. She doesn't do that. The bell rings, and Miss Hansen says, "Okay, folks," and we get our coats and go.

I put my books away and came back to Peter.

"Where do you live?" he asked.

"125 Seneca," I said.

"Where's that?" asked Peter.

"About five blocks from here," I told him. "I walk. Where's your house?"

"On Woodburn Road. You know where that is?"

Everybody knows where Woodburn Road is. It's one of the fanciest streets in Clayton, Kansas. Not many people live out there. Valerie does. Our class had a swimming party at her house last year.

"Do you have a swimming pool?" I asked.

"Yeah, sure," Peter said.

Man! I wish I had a pool. I would swim around in it every day.

The bell rang.

"Okay, folks," Miss Hansen said. Everybody ran for their lockers. Robert came by, so I thought I might as well try.

"Wanna shoot baskets after school?" I asked.

"I can't, I have to go over to this guy's house and do something," he said. I should have known.

Then Peter asked, "Do the after-school buses leave from the same place they come to in the morning?" I had forgotten how new he was.

"Yeah," I said. "I'll walk out with you if you want."

"Thanks," Peter said. He didn't say "Nah, don't bother" or "Forget it, I can find it," the way some kids would. He sounded like he wanted me to come out with him. Alison was leaving, but I knew I could catch up with her later.

Miss Hansen said, "So long, Peter. I'm glad you've come. Are you feeling settled?"

"Yes, thanks," Peter said. In the hall, he turned to me and said, "She seems nice."

"She's my best teacher so far," I told him. "You're lucky you got her. The other fifth-grade teacher is mean. She even comes in and gives Miss *Hansen* a hard time when she thinks our class is too noisy."

Peter laughed. We pushed the back doors open.

"Hey, there's my bus," he said. "Number 16. Okay, man, I'm on my way. See you tomorrow." He slapped my hand, the way guys on TV do when somebody scores.

I watched him get on the bus. I was glad I wasn't him, moving to a new school after the year had already started. Still, it didn't look as though he'd have any trouble. People will probably make friends with him. I hope he'll keep on acting like my friend, too.

I was starting to practice free throws. I had made six out of seven when Rover began barking to get out. He must have heard Mom's car. He goes crazy when she comes home. Rover's not really a Rover kind of dog. He's a little black and white spaniel.

My parents named him Rover for a joke, when I was too little to know they were just being funny. When one of us comes home, Rover goes into his routine: two flat-out turns around the house, a dash up the street, then a U-turn and back home. Then he rolls around on his back with his legs in the air. Then he jumps up on you. After that he walks toward the house like an ordinary dog, with his tail wagging.

Mom drove up the driveway.

"Hi, Stuart," she said, rolling down her window. Rover shot up the street. "How're you doing?"

"Good," I said. "I made about half my baskets lefty."

"Did you do your homework?" Mom asked. She asks me that every single afternoon.

"Not yet," I said. "I'll do it after supper." I can't see why you should do homework when it's still daylight out. Why waste good practice time?

"Well, remember the homework before you turn on the TV," Mom said.

She put the car in the garage and came out. Rover dashed back from his run up the street and jumped on her. I think maybe he likes Mom best. I guess she feeds him the most. It's supposed to be my job, but sometimes I forget.

"That's enough, Rover," Mom said. "This is my last decent pair of stockings. Come on now, get down."

I took some of Mom's books and carried them

in. Mom is a teacher, but not the ordinary kind. She goes to kids' houses to teach them when they're sick. Some of the kids just have chicken pox or sprained ankles or stuff like that, but Mom has some kids who've been sick for months or even years. She teaches one seventh-grade girl in a lung machine. The girl reads books by looking in a mirror they put up over her machine. Mom also teaches a boy in tenth grade who is paralyzed. She says he likes baseball, but he can only read about it. He can't ever play, not in his whole life. I would feel horrible to be him.

Mom stopped at the mailbox. "Your *Guidelines* came," she said, spreading the mail out on the kitchen table.

Guidelines for Children is a magazine my grandmother gives me for my birthday every year. She'll probably still be giving it to me in college! It has stories and poems and articles like "Festivals in Foreign Lands." I wish Grandma gave me *Sports Illustrated* instead.

The only good thing in *Guidelines* is the "Pen Pals Page." I read all the letters, and if there's a good one I answer it. Then the person is supposed to write back. I have a whole box of letters I got that way.

A good thing about writing to pen pals is that your letters don't have to be all true. I mean, not every single word. I always sign my real name and address, but sometimes I write about things that didn't really happen. Like how I shoot baskets with my best friend or how my brother is a basketball star. How could a pen pal find out I don't have a brother?

This month's "Pen Pals Page" wasn't so good. Most of the letters were from girls, except one from a boy who explained how to raise gerbils, which I'm not so interested in. Another one was from a kid in Missouri. I wouldn't be a pen pal to anybody that near me because he might drive through Kansas sometime and find out who I really am.

There was a honk in the driveway.

"There's Mark!" Mom said. "And I haven't even begun to think about supper."

I went out to meet Dad. He's a really tall man, six two and a half. He used to play basketball, in college. Dad's an architect. He mostly designs offices, but he designed my bedroom and all my furniture, too.

Dad was rubbing Rover's stomach with his foot. Rover was yipping with joy.

"Hi, Stuart, what's new?" Dad asked.

"There's a new kid in our class," I said. "His name is Peter. He used to live near New York City. He saw a Knicks game once."

"That's nice," Dad said. "Why don't you ask him over some afternoon?"

That's the kind of question my parents always ask. I wish they wouldn't keep saying I should have somebody over. It's so hard to explain to them! I *would* like to ask Peter over, but how could I do that until I knew for sure he would want to come? He might just think I asked him so he'd ask me back to swim in his pool.

Another kid would know what I mean. Kids understand things like that. They know you can't make a friend just because your parents want you to.

2

Teachers sometimes pick me for things, but kids in my class hardly ever do. They usually nominate someone like Chip Barnes or Valerie Allen. I don't mind that much. I think it must be pretty hard to get other people to do things, the way a chairperson has to. Anyway, I probably wouldn't get elected even if I was nominated.

So I wasn't paying much attention the next day when we had elections for chairperson of the Assembly Committee. I was reading a book about the first moon landing, where Neil Armstrong was just opening the door of the capsule. All of a sudden, somebody said my name.

"Stuart Wilson."

It was Peter!

Miss Hansen wrote my name down on the board. Other kids were pushing their arms in the air and saying, "Uh, uh!" so she would call on them. Annie nominated Valerie. Danny nominated Chip

Barnes. Then all the people who were grunting put their hands down. Nobody had any other ideas.

With Miss Hansen, everybody has to close their eyes when we vote, not just the kids who get nominated. That's the kind of teacher she is. She always wants things to be fair, and she cares about how you feel. She even cares about people in history. She's been teaching us the real truth about what the white people did to the Indians. How they took away their land and killed their buffaloes and made them move onto reservations.

Anyway, we closed our eyes, and Miss Hansen read the list of names, mine first. I wished I could see who voted for me. Peter, at least, because he nominated me. Probably Alison. Maybe Robert. When Miss Hansen said "Valerie Allen," I could tell that a lot of hands went up. The same with Chip. I voted for Chip. I would rather have voted for myself so there would be one more vote for me, but how could I do that with Miss Hansen counting? Then she would see me voting for myself. So I voted for Chip. I wouldn't vote for Valerie because she always thinks she's so great. I don't know why Alison likes her.

"All right," Miss Hansen said. "You can open your eyes."

Chip's name was the only one left on the board. Mine and Valerie's were erased.

"It was close," Miss Hansen said, looking at me. She was probably just trying to make me feel good. She always says that after we vote, anyway.

"Thanks anyhow," I said to Peter.

"Sure," he said. "Too bad you didn't win."

"That's okay," I said. I didn't tell him I don't usually get nominated, even. I'm glad Miss Hansen said it was close. Maybe it really was. Some people I didn't think of might have voted for me.

In the next week, Peter got friendly with just about everybody in our class. I knew he would. When we had to get reading partners, he asked Chip right off, "Wanna read with me?" And Chip said, "Sure."

I *hate* it when we have to choose partners. Teachers never seem to notice how often they ask you to do that, or to get into a group or make up a committee. Even Miss Hansen. They ought to understand that it's hard for some kids to do those kinds of things. I bet every single teacher wasn't popular when they were in school. They ought to remember how it feels to always worry whether someone will choose you.

Peter didn't have to worry. Everybody chose him. I was glad that he still did things with me, too. He came over and sat next to me when we had a class meeting about our assembly program. It was a pretty dumb meeting. Nobody had good ideas. Annie suggested a talent show, as usual. She has this talent, ballet dancing, and she always wants to show off. She did a solo dance called "A French Pirouette" in our Songs Around the World assembly last year. It was exactly the same dance she did the year before that, only then she called it "The Dance of the Snowflake" because that assembly was about winter. She wore the same dress both years. It had about ten petticoats. Last year it was getting small, and her underpants showed. Robert told me, and I looked and he was right.

Robert suggested Olden Times in Clayton, but everybody's tired of Olden Times. Valerie wanted a play about myths. Danny suggested a Plains Indian pageant. That sounded pretty good. We could do things we already knew, like the Buffalo Dance.

The trouble with democratic discussions is that they take so long. Kids were starting to act crazy, punching each other and laughing. Robert got up and came over to the pencil sharpener in back of me.

"Hey, Robert, wanna come to my house and shoot some baskets after school?" I asked him while he was there.

"Sure, maybe," Robert said. "I don't know, though."

That's the way he is. He won't say yes or no. You never can tell whether he'll do what you ask him to or not.

"Well, do you think you will?" I asked.

"Hey, you guys!" Chip shouted. "Sit down, you're holding things up." Chip always acts so bossy. I don't know why people always want him for chairperson.

So we took a vote, and I still didn't know about

Robert. Anyway, the Plains Indian program won. That should be okay. Maybe I could work on the scenery.

"I've already made a tepee model," I told Peter.

"That one on the table in back?" he asked. "It's neat."

Suddenly I thought, why not ask *Peter* over. He sure acts a lot more friendly than Robert. But I couldn't ask him for that afternoon, in case Robert did come. So I said, "Hey, want to come over to my house tomorrow and shoot baskets?"

"I can't," Peter said. "I have to go to the dentist. Some other time, though."

I didn't know if he was just saying that, or what. I didn't really expect him to say yes. Anyway, I asked.

The rest of the day we worked on our metric project. Miss Hansen thinks we should learn the metric system because almost all other countries use it and our country might change to it. We're making a graph of everyone's height in centimeters. It's lucky we didn't start to plot it before Peter came. That afternoon we measured him, and guess what? He was 156 centimeters tall, the *exact same* height as me!

"Hey! So'm I!" I said.

"You could be twins," said Alison, "except Peter's dark and you're blond."

"Well, sometimes twins look different," I said.

Peter watched us start to plot the heights.

"It looks funny in centimeters," he said.

"You get used to it," I told him. "I can think in centimeters now, without having to work it out in inches first."

Alison said, "Like, I bet Miss Hansen is about, uh, 170 centimeters."

"How tall is that in inches?" asked Peter.

We explained that that's what you're not supposed to ask. You can't go around multiplying and changing in your head all the time. You have to learn to think in meters right off.

Just then the door opened, and this man I'd never seen before came in and looked around and went over to Miss Hansen.

"Dad!" Peter said. He ran over to them. The man smiled at Peter and put his arm around him and leaned down and said something.

Peter came back to us.

"How come your father's here?" I asked.

"He's taking me to the dentist," Peter said.

He just told me he had to go to the dentist *tomorrow*. I wonder if he was just making that up.

The bell rang, and Miss Hansen looked up and said, "Okay, folks, but pick up a little, please, if you've been working on a project."

I went up to Robert. "You coming over, or not?"

"I don't know," he said. "Probably, I'll see."

It sure is a drag to get anything out of him.

We all started getting our jackets and packing up our books.

15

"See you tomorrow," Peter said, going out the door with his father.

I knew he was saying it to everybody. But I answered.

"See you tomorrow."

3

I walked fast to catch up to Alison. Then I sneaked up behind her and sort of bopped her on the head with my book, like I always do.

Alison turned around fast. "Cut it out, Stuart!" she said, like she always does.

We walked on down School Street and turned into Seneca.

"Guess what?" Alison asked. "My father's going to put up a basketball hoop!"

"He is?" I asked. I was surprised. Mr. Henning usually pays more attention to Alison's little brother. I think he likes Jimmy better than Alison.

"It's really for Jimmy," Alison said. "My father wants to get him interested in basketball."

"That's crazy!" I said. "He's only three years old!"

"I know it," she said. "But my dad wants to get things ready for him. Anyway, it's good because now I'll be able to practice whenever I want. You can come over and play too."

"Thanks," I said. It might be good to practice at Alison's sometimes. It doesn't usually bother me to have her watch. In fact, sometimes it seems like I shoot better when she's there. And her dad will probably buy a good hoop because of Jimmy. You would think he would at least say it was partly for her.

Jimmy was outside, on his tricycle.

"Hi, Alison. Hi, Stuart," he called. "Wanna see me go in a circle?"

Then he started riding around in circles. He can really go fast. Alison caught his handlebars and made him stop and hugged him. Jimmy laughed.

Alison asked if I wanted to come in and see an afternoon special on TV with her. I said I couldn't because of Robert.

"Are you going to Robert's Halloween party?" Alison asked.

"No," I said. I didn't know Robert was going to have a Halloween party! Kids in our class usually go trick-or-treating on their own streets. Alison takes Jimmy around before supper, and then we go out together when it's dark. Anyway, that's what we used to do.

"Guess what, Alison?" Jiimmy started. But I didn't let him interrupt.

"Are you?" I asked.

"Am I what?" Alison said.

"Going to Robert's party."

"Nope," she said.

"How come?" I asked.

"He didn't *ask* me," Alison said. "I just heard him telling Danny he might have one." She didn't seem to care. I don't think she worries about things like that.

"Maybe Robert was just making it up," she said. "He does that. He always wants you to think he has lots of friends and all."

I wondered if that was true.

Jimmy was jumping up and down. "Alison!" he yelled. "I'm going to Larry's for supper!"

Larry is his friend. He lives around the corner.

"That's nice," Alison said.

"Hey, Stuart, I'm going to Larry's for supper!" Jimmy told me, as though I hadn't already heard him.

"That's good, Jimmy," I said. "So long, Alison."

Just then, Rover came charging up the street to meet me. I caught him before he made his usual U-turn. He wriggled in my arms, whapping his tail against me.

"Good old Rover," I said, putting my face down into his soft fur. "You're some good old dog." Rover even smells good, in a dog kind of way. Sort of woolly and warm.

"C'mon, I'll race you home," I told him. I run fast, but I can never beat Rover. He was waiting for me on the porch when I got there.

Usually I like to be alone in my house after school. I take my time, fix a snack and read or just sit and think about things. This afternoon was different, though. I didn't want to eat anything till Robert came, if he came. Then I'd get a good big snack for the two of us. But the thing was, I wasn't sure he'd come, and I was hungry. So I took a banana from the bowl and ate that.

It was a quarter of four. If Robert was coming, he would be here pretty soon. I went upstairs to change.

My room is the whole third floor of our house. You could make two rooms or even three little ones out of that much space. But my dad made it all into one big room for me. I have basketball pictures on one whole wall and a Knicks banner over my bed. My room is so big that I could have a basket on the door and practice inside in bad weather, except my parents won't let me. Part of their bedroom is under mine, and they say I thump around enough as it is.

When I went back downstairs it was four o'clock. I sat down in the kitchen and tightened the laces on my new Adidas that my dad got me. They're the shoes all the pros wear.

Then I went out. Rover came too. He likes to watch me practice. I tell him to sit and he does, but his butt never really touches the ground. He's always ready to take off and run if Mom or Dad should come home.

I started to practice. I wanted to try dribbling in a zigzag pattern up to the basket, with a pivot halfway there. If you get a maneuver like that down smooth, you can outwit any defense. I started way down the driveway near the street and pivoted when I got near the front of the house. Then I dribbled right up to the basket and shot. Two points! I went back down the driveway and did it again.

Each time I scored, I looked around to see if Robert was coming up the street. But he never was. I decided I better go in and look at the clock. I tried some free throws first, to take up more time, and then I went in. Four-thirty! I ate another banana. Then I went out again. I missed my first shot, but the second sank in just perfect.

"Beautiful!" somebody said.

I turned around. It was Alison, with Jimmy holding her hand.

"I'm going to Larry's!" Jimmy yelled. "For supper!"

"Yeah," I said. "I heard."

Now Alison would see that Robert hadn't come. Jimmy pulled at her. He was really excited about Larry's. It doesn't take much to please a little kid. It wouldn't take so much to make me feel good, either. Like Robert coming up the street just when I made a basket.

I called after Jimmy, "Have fun."

"See ya when I come back," called Alison.

I went on with my practice. I was really getting

hot. I could just hear the announcer calling my moves: "Wilson runs forward for the rebound, catches it, pivots, shoots—he makes it! A terrific shot that ties up the score! They're going wild here in New York tonight, folks!"

It was probably about a quarter to five. Now I knew for sure that Robert wouldn't come. I wonder why? Maybe he had to do something for his mother. Maybe he really wants to come over, but she won't let him. I wonder if that's why. Anyway, I should try asking Peter again. He sounded like he wanted to come, except for the dentist. I bet he really does have to go two days in a row. Sometimes you do.

"Hey, Stuart, pass it!" Alison called, coming back up the driveway. I threw her the ball. She caught it on the bounce and dribbled up to me. I jumped around to guard her, but she pivoted and shot fast. The ball went right in.

"Hey, did you see that?" she yelled, running after the rebound.

"Yeah, good shot," I said, grabbing it ahead of her. I shot fast and missed.

"Oh, man!" I said. "That's about the first one I've missed all afternoon." I caught the ball on the bounce and held on to it.

"I know. You were really hot before," Alison said. "Well, I have to go home and help Mom get supper. See ya, Stuart."

"See ya," I said.

I was glad she didn't say anything about Robert.

Suddenly Rover jumped up and took off around the house. Mom's car turned into the driveway.

She parked, got out, and pulled her books off the seat.

"Hi, hon," she said. "How was your day?"

"Okay," I said.

"Anyone come over?"

"Nah. I just hung out by myself." I followed her up the steps. Rover was still up the block somewhere. Mom went in.

"You'll miss Rover," I said.

"Good!" She put her books on the table and sat down with her coat on. All of a sudden she began to cry. Mom hardly ever cries. I touched her hair. "Are you okay, Mom?"

"I'm okay," she said, reaching up for my hand. "I'm sorry, Stuart. I just feel so bad."

"Did something happen?" I asked.

"I had a tough day, and at the end I went to see Robbie Holmes." Robbie's the boy who's paralyzed. "He's so close to his father. Now it turns out that the Holmeses are getting a divorce. Poor Robbie had to tell me this afternoon. I gave him a book to show his father, and he said, 'Mrs. Wilson, Dad's leaving home.' "

"That's sad," I said.

"It is," said Mom. "And it's a terrible burden on a family to live with a sickness like Robbie's for so many years, day in and day out. I don't see how people bear it, honestly I don't."

I think Mom is good to help other people the

way she does. When you think about all the problems the kids she knows have, it seems pretty crazy for me to feel bad about a little thing like Robert not coming over.

After supper that night I went upstairs to do my homework. Then I realized that I had left my science book at school. So I figured I would write to a pen pal instead. That's good writing practice, so if Mom asked me if I was doing homework, I could say yes and it would be sort of true.

I took out the two letters I hadn't answered yet and read them over. I decided not to write back to John Hoberman from Miami, Florida, because after he signed his name, he wrote "age nine." I don't care how old he is, but that's a dumb way to tell you. The other letter was from Marty Goldman in Lansing, Michigan. He has a brother, two dogs, three cats, and a parakeet with a bald spot where some feathers came out. His letter said, "Last Saturday I went on a hike with some other kids. We took one of my dogs, the one called Zip. We put our sandwich stuff next to a tree and went to get water. When we came back, Zip had eaten up all the sandwiches except for some bread. Boy, were we mad! Well, I hope you are fine. Please write back again."

I decided to answer that one. I pulled out my pad of yellow paper that Dad brings me from his office and began.

Dear Marty,

That was funny about your dog eating up the sandwiches. I guess you didn't think it was so funny then, though!! I have been pretty busy, which is why I didn't write back sooner. This afternoon my friend Robert came over to shoot baskets, the way he always does. He is pretty good but (not to boast) I almost always beat him. I am practicing shooting lefty. (I am right-handed.) I have a new friend from New York City, named Peter. He used to live right next to the Empire State Building. He moved here to a house with a swimming pool. I can go swimming over there whenever I want. Well, I have to stop now. Write back soon.

Your friend,
Stu Wilson

I didn't have an envelope, so I left the letter out on my desk where I'd see it and remember to mail it later.

"Stuart," Mom called up the steps, "have you finished your homework?"

"Just about," I said.

"About bedtime?" Dad called.

"Yep," I said. "I'm just going."

"Sleep well," Dad said.

I lay in bed and listened to them talking downstairs. I knew Dad would be able to make Mom feel better, just by listening. In a way, they're like each other's best friend.

After a while, I went to sleep.

4

I once read in some book that too much noise can make a person deaf, or crazy, or even dead. The person who wrote that ought to eat lunch in our school cafeteria. It's so noisy in there you have to yell real loud just to tell somebody to shut up. And the back of the cafeteria where our class eats is getting noisier all the time.

For one thing, the girls always yell over to the boys' table. Then some of the guys usually jump up and punch the girls or grab their lunch bags. People are always knocking over benches, trying to change tables before the lunch aide makes them go back. Every day somebody's milk gets spilled.

I think some girls in our class are starting to want to be girlfriends with the guys. The other day, Chip yelled something about Annie's big feet tripping her up when she dances, and Annie jumped right up from the girls' table and smiled at Chip like he had said something nice! Then she squeezed in next to him on the bench and grabbed his chocolate milk and sat there and drank all of it.

I always used to sit at the end of the boys' table. But these days you never know what table to sit at because the girls and the guys are getting all mixed up. Since Peter came, I've been trying to go and sit next to him. It's fun to eat with Peter. He tells lots of good stories about his old school. But this day when I came in, Peter was already sitting with Chip and Valerie and Annie, and there wasn't any more room. So I had to take my lunch bag and milk and go over to the other table where Robert was eating. I wondered if he would explain why he didn't come over yesterday, but I wasn't going to ask.

I opened my sandwich, which was cheese and lettuce on whole wheat bread. I like the lunches Mom makes, but I just wish she'd break down and buy cookies once! Anyway, Mom's lunches are a lot better than the cafeteria's. Mom says our cafeteria is the only place she knows where they call spaghetti a vegetable. If the menu says "meat loaf and vegetable," the vegetable is usually spaghetti. The spaghetti is soft and slimy. Most kids in our class bring lunch.

Alison sat down across from us. "All right!" she said, looking in her bag. "Bacon, lettuce, and tomato. My favorite. And chocolate chip cookies."

I love Alison's mother's chocolate chip cookies. She always used to give us cookies and milk when I was little and went to Alison's nearly every day.

"Want one, Stuart?" Alison asked.

Just then Valerie jumped up from the other table, waving Chip's lunch bag in the air.

"Alison, catch!" she yelled. "Catch!"

She tossed the bag to Alison. It was a bad throw. Alison missed, and the bag broke open on the floor. An orange rolled under my feet.

Valerie jumped up and started scrambling around under me. "Look out, Wilson," she said, pushing my feet aside.

Chip just stood there, mumbling, "Hey, my lunch . . ."

I tried to reach the orange, but it rolled over to Alison's side. Alison got it and took it over to the other table and gave it to Valerie.

"It looks just delicious!" Valerie said as she began to peel it slowly. "Absolutely delicious!" Then she passed pieces of Chip's orange along the table. All the girls took a piece.

I thought about taking one of the cookies Alison had left. After all, she'd already offered me one. But I didn't.

At the other table, Valerie wiped her mouth with her napkin in little dabs. "That was a gorgeous snack," she said in a high voice. "Thank you so much, Chip, *dear*."

"Valerie acts like a dope," Robert said. Then he sort of laughed and changed the subject. "I bet you waited for me to come over yesterday."

"Yeah," I said. I wasn't going to give him any more satisfaction than that.

"Well, I couldn't," Robert said. "I had to do some stuff."

I said, "Oh." I guess he was probably trying to apologize.

I pulled out a carrot stick and bit into it. It tasted good, but I didn't feel so hot. Partly because of Robert. Partly the other stuff, about girlfriends and all that.

I don't really understand about girlfriends. I don't even know what you're supposed to do to get one. Whether you're supposed to *ask* somebody or if they just know when they are. All of a sudden, it seems like everybody but me knows about stuff like that. Another thing I don't know is what you're supposed to do if you *have* a girlfriend. I hope you aren't supposed to hug and kiss and stuff like that all the time. I wouldn't mind it now and then, but most of the time I would rather shoot baskets. In a way, it seems like it's a lot of trouble to get yourself a girlfriend.

Still, I wish I could kid around with girls the way Chip does. Or even just act regular, like Peter. I looked at the other table, where Peter was laughing with Valerie.

Then I realized Robert was still talking to me. "Well, maybe some other time," he said.

It sounded like he wanted me to ask him over again. But I was just about fed up. Why should I keep asking if he's never going to come? I just wished somebody would ask *me*, for a change.

Just then, like I had rubbed a magic lamp or something, it happened! Peter came by with his tray.

"Hey, Stuart," he asked. "Can you come over to my house on Thursday?"

All right! "Sure, I guess so," I said.

"That'll be the first day so far I don't have to go to the dentist," he said.

"How come you go so much?" I asked. I was glad to know that he really did have to go that other day when I asked him over.

"I'm getting braces," Peter said. He opened his mouth and pointed to his front teeth. "See, this tooth sort of crosses over that one. Listen," he went on, "be sure to bring your bathing suit to school on Thursday. If it's warm, we can go swimming."

I said okay. Man, was that going to be neat!

"Wait till you ride my bus," Peter said. "There are these sixth-grade girls on it who sing dirty songs, and the bus driver doesn't even make them stop."

That sounded interesting. I was really glad Peter asked me. See, that proves it was worth trying, when I asked him over before.

After lunch we had gym, and right in front of everybody, I made three free throws. I felt so good!

When we went back to the room, Alison came over. "I saved you a cookie, Stuart," she said. She gave it to me. Good thing I hadn't just taken one before.

"I made three free throws in gym," I told Alison, biting into the cookie.

"You're so lucky to get basketball in school," she said. "We had a dumb field hockey game. Half the time we just stood around."

Valerie was standing near us. "Yeah, it isn't fair," she said. "We have fun with Miss Hansen, but it's not the same as having Coach Schultz teach us." She shook her hair out of her eyes and made a face.

The bell rang.

"Going home?" Alison asked. She asks me that every day, even though I always say yes. I was going to feel good on Thursday, when I could say I was going to Peter's.

"Yeah, let's go."

Alison and I went out the door. I saw Robert hanging around, sort of waiting, but I didn't say anything to him. Then he walked off to his bus by himself.

Alison and I walked along nice and slow, the way we usually do. The trees were beginning to turn yellow. I always like it when fall comes along—you get Halloween and Thanksgiving, and then it's not so long till Christmas.

"We're going to get the backboard Saturday," Alison said. "I hope Dad puts it up right away. Then you can come over and try it."

"Sure," I said. "Unless I'm at Peter's or something." I couldn't help saying it, just to let Alison know.

"Oh, sure," Alison said quickly. "I mean, you

could come over if you didn't have anything else to do."

Right then, when Alison and I turned onto Seneca Street, I suddenly realized something. It might sound crazy. I mean, how come I never noticed before, after all the days Alison and I walked home together? But the whole idea just came to me, by surprise, that afternoon.

I bet Alison likes me.

5

In a way, I wish I got to take a bus to school. Peter's bus was neat. Valerie's the only person from our class besides Peter on it. There were lots of little kids. The big kids sat in back and fooled around together. Peter and I sat on the long back seat next to a couple of sixth graders. Peter seemed to be friends with them already. He sure makes friends fast.

Valerie turned around. "What are *you* doing on this bus, Wilson?" she asked.

"Going to Peter's," I said.

"Oh," said Valerie. She looked as though she was trying to think of something funny to say, but she couldn't. "Well, oh, boy," she said.

That's how lots of kids talk when they try to act cool. I'm not so good at it. It's one reason I usually feel shy with Valerie. When I feel good, I get excited and I forget to be cool. Right then I was excited about going to Peter's.

"Do you have a brother or sister?" I asked him.

"A brother in ninth grade," he said, "and a little sister. She's three."

"You're lucky," I said. "What's your brother's name?"

"Geoffrey. He just got on the football team," Peter said.

The girls in front of us started singing that song about ninety-nine bottles of beer: "Take one down, pass it around, ninety-eight bottles of beer on the wall," and all that.

"I thought you said they sing dirty songs," I said.

"They did yesterday," said Peter.

It seemed like I picked the wrong day to ride Peter's bus. I wondered what songs they sang yesterday.

The bus pulled over to a corner and stopped. Everybody kept on talking and laughing. Then Valerie let out a little yell: "Ooh, it's my stop!" She pulled her books off the floor by the book strap, climbed over a couple of girls, and ran down the aisle. Halfway down, she sort of wiggled her butt. All the girls yelled and laughed.

"C'mon, get a move on," the driver called. "You're holding everyone up."

Valerie looked back down the aisle and waved. Then she jumped down.

"She sure thinks she's pretty great," I said.

"She's okay," Peter said. "Her mother, too."

I was surprised. "How do you know?"

"Last week they both came over and brought us this big cheesecake, because we just moved to the neighborhood."

"Well, that must have been her mother's idea," I said. "You don't think Valerie went out and bought the cheesecake with her own money, do you?"

"No. But still . . ." Peter said.

I didn't say anything. I hoped Peter wouldn't get too friendly with Valerie.

"My stop's next," Peter said. "Get your stuff ready."

There were only two houses on Peter's block—a white one with pillars and a brown one with glass windows and a deck all around it. It looked like a house Dad showed me once in a book he has. I hoped it was Peter's.

"Which one's yours?" I asked.

"The brown one," Peter said.

We walked up the gravel path. It crunched when we stepped on it. There were little trees in pots by the front door.

"Where's your pool?" I asked.

"Out back," Peter said. "Come in and meet Mom, and then we can swim if she lets us. She always says it's too cold, but she usually lets us go in anyway."

"She sounds like my mom," I said.

Peter rang the bell. It made a *bing-bong* chiming sound.

The whole front door was glass, so I could see right inside. There were iron steps going upstairs and a hallway through to the back. I could see a little bit of the edge of the pool.

Nobody came. Peter rang again.

Someone called, "I'll be right there."

I looked through the side window into the living room. It looked like the kind you see in magazines. There was a big white rug and two white couches. A really big picture was hanging on the wall.

Then a woman came downstairs carrying a little girl in overalls. I was surprised. I knew Peter's family was rich, but I didn't expect them to have a maid. Peter hadn't said anything about that. This maid was a pretty black woman with real short hair and big earrings. She smiled at us through the glass and opened the door.

"Hi, Mom," Peter said. "Here's Stuart."

She was Peter's mother.

"Hi, Peter," she said. "Hi, Stuart. I'm glad to meet you." She smiled and held the door open for us with the arm that wasn't around the girl. "Come on in," she said. "You'll have to make your own snack, Peter. I can't seem to get Diane to wake up. She's been asleep for two hours." She led us into the kitchen.

I was so surprised that Peter's mother was black that I couldn't think of anything to say.

"Put your things on the table," Peter said in the kitchen. "Is there lemonade, Mom?"

"Sure," Peter's mother said. "Take what you want, lemonade or orange juice. There's peanut butter and jam, too." She smiled at me. "If you're like Peter," she said, "you're hungry."

"Yeah," I said. "Yes, I am. Thanks." Maybe she didn't notice I was surprised.

Peter was taking things out of the refrigerator. His mother sat down at the table and pulled out a chair for me with her free hand. "Sit down, Stuart, and tell me about school. One reason we decided to live in Clayton was because of the schools."

I sat down. My whole face felt hot. I wondered if Peter's mother could tell that at first I thought she was the maid. But how could she, unless she could read minds or something?

I watched Peter whizzing the lemonade in the blender. The blender made a lot of noise, and I didn't have to say anything. Peter's sister raised her head off her mother's shoulder and looked at me. Then she put her face right back down. She had little damp curls at the back of her neck. Her hair was black. Her neck was sort of light brown.

The blender stopped.

"Diane, aren't you going to say hello to Stuart?" her mother asked.

Diane shook her head.

"Hi, Diane," I said.

"Say hi," Peter told her. He put two glasses of lemonade on the table. "Want one, Mom?"

"Not now, thanks," his mother said. "I'll wait and see what this girl is going to do."

"I want lemonade!" Diane said. She climbed off her mother's lap, pulled out a chair, and climbed up on it. "Lemonade!" she said. She reminded me of Jimmy.

"Okay, okay," Peter said. He got a plastic cup and poured lemonade halfway up.

Then the doorbell rang.

"There's Geoff," Mrs. Baker said. She went out to the door.

"Want a peanut butter sandwich?" Peter asked.

"Sure," I said. It was good to have something to do, like eat.

Peter took out plates, and the bread and jam, and two jars of peanut butter.

"Which do you want, smooth or chunky?"

"Smooth," I said.

"Same here," said Peter. "I hate that chunky. It gets stuck in your teeth."

"Yeah," I said. "I don't see why they even make it." I felt a little bit better. I really like conversations where you tell your opinions.

"Because some idiots like it," Peter said. "Like Geoffrey," he added, real loud.

"Who're you calling an idiot?" yelled Geoffrey, coming into the kitchen. "You wanna take that back?" He grabbed Peter around the neck and grinned down at him. "Take it back?"

Peter pretended to gurgle and choke. He raised

his hand. Geoffrey let go. "Give me some of that good old chunky, man," he said to Peter. "And any lemonade you got left." Then he sat down across from me.

"Hi," he said.

You could tell he was Peter's brother. He looked like Peter, only darker. He had curly hair like Peter and Diane.

"Geoffrey, Geoffrey," yelled Diane, banging her cup on the table.

"Hello, cutie-pie," said Geoffrey. "What's new?"

Peter's mom said, "She slept for two full hours, and now she's so full of energy she can't sit still. I'm afraid you boys are going to have her trailing around after you."

"Not me," said Geoffrey. "I've gotta go work on the lawn. I promised Dad."

"We're going swimming," Peter said. He didn't sound too sure. He looked at his mother.

"Oh, are you sure you really want to, on a day like this?" she asked, just like my mom. "Stuart, are you sure that's what you'd like?"

"Definitely," I said. "I brought my suit." I hoped she would let us go.

"Well, you'd better get out there fast, then, while there's still some sun left," she said. That meant we could go!

"Go swimming!" Diane shouted.

"Not today," said her mother. "It's too chilly for you. Let's read a book together."

"Swimming!" yelled Diane. She jumped around on the kitchen floor, pulling her mother's leg.

"Come on, Stuart," Peter said. "We better get out of here."

We went down the hall to Peter's room to put on our suits. His room was cool. One whole wall was glass. He had travel posters of New York City on the other wall and some model planes on his desk.

Peter said, "You can change in the bathroom."

I was glad, because I don't really like to change my clothes in front of people. Peter opened a door I thought was a closet. There was this whole bathroom, just for him. It had red towels and a red rug. The toilet and bathtub and washbasin were gray. I never saw a fancy bathroom like that before.

I took off my clothes and pulled on my suit. I took a long time, so I could think about everything that had happened.

Peter tossed me a towel, and we went outside.

There was a cement walk around the pool, with big chairs to lie on and some flowerpots at the edge. Behind the pool, the yard just turned into a field. You could see a long way off. That's a neat thing about Kansas. You can see so far. I don't see why Montana gets to be called the Big Sky Country. I bet the sky in Kansas is just as big.

"Wanna go off the diving board?" Peter asked.

"No, I'll just jump in," I said. I held my nose

and ran across the cement and jumped. Cold! Was it cold!

Peter jumped in after me. We splashed around some, and then we had a race to the other side, which I won. Then we played tag for a while. After that we treaded water. I was shivering.

"Let's get out," Peter said.

We swam over to the ladder and climbed up. I grabbed my towel and rubbed myself all over and wrapped the towel around me. Peter did the same. Then we lay down on two big chairs next to each other. My fingers were all puckered up from the water. I was shaking some, but getting warmer. It felt good to lie there, wrapped in a thick towel, watching the clouds float along way up in the sky. It felt good to be with a friend.

"Do you like it in Kansas?" I asked.

"Yeah," Peter said. "Except it seems funny that everything's so flat."

That never bothered me. I guess it *is* flat here, but that's how I like it. Still, if you were used to something else . . .

We watched the clouds move along.

"It looks like they're going about a hundred miles an hour," Peter said.

"Yeah," I said. I always think that.

We lay there for a while. Then Peter said, "Let's go in. I'm still cold."

I was too. I guess Peter's mother was right. It *was* a pretty cold day to go swimming. But it was fun, anyway.

6

When we were dressed, Peter showed me his airplane models. He made them with his father. It turns out his father's an aeronautical engineer at MacKnight Aviation. The reason they moved here is because Peter's father got this special job where he's in charge of inventing a new kind of jet engine.

By this time I felt more comfortable. It felt like I could say anything and it would be okay with Peter.

"I didn't know your mother was black," I said.

"Yeah," Peter said.

"And your father's white," I said.

"Yeah."

Peter's bed was like a couch, with big pillows against the wall. I leaned back.

"It seems like everybody in your family's some different color."

"So?" Peter said. I couldn't tell if he was mad.

"Nothing," I said. "I was surprised, that's all. I didn't expect it."

"Lots of people didn't expect it," Peter said. "Some people around here act like they've never seen a black person before."

I haven't seen many black people, except when I went to a Bulls game in Kansas City. But I didn't want to say so.

"Some dumb kids in Geoffrey's school called him a nigger," Peter said.

Oh, man! "Well, what some dopes say can't hurt you," I said. "They're just dumb, that's all."

"Yeah," said Peter. "But I'm scared Geoff's going to get in a fight. He says these kids have been trailing him home and downtown and at the field and everywhere. He won't tell Mom and Dad because he doesn't want to worry them."

"That's awful, when you just moved here and all," I said.

"Yeah," Peter said.

We sat there for a while. I didn't feel like I had to say anything. What Peter told me was terrible. But I was glad he told me.

After a while, Peter asked, "Do you have brothers or sisters?"

"No, there's just me," I said. I hate to say that. People always ask how come, and I don't know what to answer.

But Peter didn't say anything.

"My parents just wanted one kid," I told him.

That's how I usually explain it. I hoped Peter wouldn't think my parents were mean or hated kids or something.

"It must be neat, just having three people," he said.

That's just what I always wish people would say. I was beginning to feel good, hanging out with Peter.

We dealt out money for Monopoly, but then my mom called and said she was coming and we should listen for her honk. So we put the money away again.

"I have a set," I said. "We could play at my house next time."

Peter said okay, and then my mother honked and I grabbed my jacket and suit and ran to the hall. Peter's mother was standing there with Diane.

"Thanks for the visit, Mrs. Baker," I said. "I had a good time."

"Come again, Stuart," she said, smiling.

"Bye, Stuart," Diane said. I waved at her through the glass.

"Have a nice visit?" Mom asked while I belted up.

"It was okay," I said.

I guess it was the best visit I'd ever had, but I didn't feel like telling her all about it.

———

I set the table while Mom cooked supper. Then Dad came home, and we sat down to eat.

"Isn't this the day you were going to visit your friend?" Dad asked.

"Yeah."

"How did it go?"

"Okay," I said. "Good."

My parents seemed to be waiting. They always want to hear about everything. I decided to tell them.

"Peter has a pool," I said. "We went swimming. His mom's black and his dad's white."

My parents looked surprised.

"It's good to meet different kinds of families," Dad began.

"Some guys called Peter's brother a nigger," I said.

"Oh, Stuart!" Mom put down her fork. "That makes me so *mad*! You'd think, in this day and age—" She turned to Dad. "I thought people in Clayton learned something, back when the Brandts adopted Lin."

"What happened then?" I asked. Lin Brandt is a girl in about tenth grade. Her family goes to our church. She's Korean or something. Her parents adopted her when she was a baby.

"Some of the neighbors got upset," Dad said, "and said things they regretted later. It was hard on the Brandts at the time."

"It was terrible!" Mom said. "But at least I thought people learned something from it. It's depressing to find out there's still prejudice in Clayton."

"It was just one kid, Mom," I said. "Most people probably aren't prejudiced."

"That's right," Dad said. "A few may be upset because a family like Peter's is new to them. But they'll get used to it."

I hope so. I couldn't help thinking about Alison's father. It's hard for him to get used to anything new—even his own daughter playing basketball.

"You know what Mr. Henning did?" I said. "He put up a hoop and told Alison it was for Jimmy! I think he's prejudiced against girls in sports."

"He may change his mind," Mom said. "The news at the teachers' meeting was that from now on boys and girls will have P. E. together in elementary school. It's a new ruling."

"All right!" I said. As soon as I said it, I wasn't so sure. Anyway, Alison will like it, I thought.

Mom went on, "And in junior high, shop and home ec are going to be integrated. Boys and girls will take both of them, together."

"You mean I'll have to take home *ec*?" I hate to cook.

Mom laughed. "Now who's afraid of something new? Don't worry, you'll probably enjoy it. Just because your father can't boil an egg—"

She always teases him about that.

Dad laughed and got up to make instant coffee. "Give me time," he said. "I'm still learning."

"Coach Schultz didn't say anything about different P. E.," I said. "Or Miss Hansen either."

"They will," Mom said. "They just found out about it yesterday. You'll be hearing soon." She put a bowl of oranges on the table.

I punched my thumb into my orange and peeled the skin down, thinking about everything that had happened. For one day, there was a lot to think about.

7

All of a sudden it was Halloween. Safeway had been full of candy corn and stuff for weeks, but I hadn't paid much attention. I guess it doesn't seem so important when you get older.

Miss Hansen read us a neat story about the headless horseman, but otherwise we didn't do much about Halloween in school. I didn't see Robert talking to anybody about his party. I bet he wasn't even having one. I didn't really care anymore. Why should I worry about Robert, now that I'm friends with Peter?

I asked Peter what he was going to do for Halloween, thinking maybe he could come over. He still hadn't been to my house, because of the dentist and stuff. Peter said he was taking Diane around in the afternoon.

"Then Geoff's going to baby-sit her at night," he said, "and my mom and dad are taking me to the movies."

"Hey, neat," I said.

"They like to go out with just one of us some-times," he said. "Last Saturday Dad took Geoff to a K.U. football game." He looked at me. "I think they want me and Geoff to have something to do tonight so we won't get into any trouble."

"Oh," I said. It must be awful to have to worry about stuff like that all the time.

"What are you doing?" asked Peter.

"I don't know yet," I said. "I usually go around with Alison." It might really be fun to go out with her this year.

When we walked home, Alison told me she was taking Jimmy out before dark.

"Wanna go out ourselves after supper?" she asked.

"Maybe," I said.

"Well, only if you feel like it," said Alison. She sounded sort of hurt. I thought about how mad I feel when Robert says "maybe" like that. I wouldn't want Alison to feel that way.

"Well, sure, let's," I said. "What should we be?"

"I was thinking I could be a gypsy," said Alison. "I could wear a dress of my mother's and lots of beads and stuff."

"I could borrow some of Dad's clothes and be a hobo," I said. "I could draw a mustache with my mother's eyebrow pencil."

"Neat," said Alison. "I'll come by after supper, okay?"

"Okay," I said. Then I decided to tell her what I'd been meaning to say, only I hadn't gotten around to it.

"Guess what," I said. "Peter's mother is black."

"She *is*?" Alison stopped on the sidewalk and grabbed my arm. "Are you sure?"

"Of course I'm sure," I said. "I *saw* her."

"But his father's white," said Alison. "I saw him, that day in school."

"Yeah," I said.

We walked on a little way. Then Alison said, "Does anyone know?"

"I guess so," I said. "Sure. I mean, all you would have to do is look."

"Yeah," she said. "Boy, I feel sorry for Peter."

"Why should you?" I asked. That made me mad. What did she know about it? "His family's nice. They have this neat house." I wished I could explain how they were just like any family, except most families don't look like them.

"What do his brother and sister look like?" Alison asked. "Like Peter? I mean he looks just like an ordinary person."

"He *is* an ordinary person!" I said. It *was* sort of complicated. "His brother's in ninth grade. His little sister's cute. She reminds me of Jimmy, the way she acts."

"Boy," Alison said, "I bet some people aren't going to like this."

"*What* people?" I asked.

"Well, like my dad," Alison said. "He doesn't like black people. I mean, he doesn't know any, but he doesn't like them anyway."

I knew it! "He'll just have to change his mind," I said.

"I guess so," Alison said. "Boy."

Jimmy was waiting for us. "Hey, Stuart, I'm gonna be an astronaut!" he said.

"That's good," I said. "I'll be looking for you."

Rover dashed up the street past me and then dashed back home. When I got there, he was running around the house, yipping. I let him in and gave him an extra big bowl of food, because of Halloween. It's a bad day for him. We always put him in the basement so he won't go wild every time the doorbell rings.

Mom had set out a bowl of apples and some boxes of raisins by the front door. She won't buy candy, even for Halloween. It's sort of embarrassing.

The doorbell rang. Then it rang again. I opened the door, and it was Jimmy. He was wearing a space suit with a plastic helmet. He had on a black cat mask under the helmet. I guess that was left over from last year.

"Hi, Stuart," he said. "Trick or treat."

Little kids just say that. They never have any trick.

I held out the bowl of apples and a box of raisins. Jimmy took an apple.

"Guess who I am?" he asked, as if I couldn't tell.

"Are you Larry?" I asked.

"No!" he said.

"Alison?"

"No!" Jimmy yelled. He pulled the mask up. "It's me!"

"Jimmy!" I said, pretending to be surprised. "You sure fooled me!"

Jimmy laughed and ran down the steps. I watched him go off with Alison, showing her his apple. I bet he told her he fooled me. Little kids are like that. They'll believe anything.

When Mom got home, all the raisin boxes were gone and only a few apples were left. We let Rover out for a break before the nighttime trick-or-treating began.

At supper, I told Mom and Dad I was going trick-or-treating with Alison.

"Can I wear your old red shirt?" I asked Dad. "And a pair of your painting pants?"

"Sure," said Dad.

"What about homework?" asked Mom.

"Miss Hansen didn't give us any, because of Halloween," I told her.

I was upstairs putting on Dad's shirt and pants when the doorbell rang.

"Stuart, Alison's here," called Mom.

"Just a sec," I called down. "I just have to make my mustache."

"Why don't you let Alison do it for you?" Mom asked. "Shall I send her up?"

"Okay," I called, without even stopping to think whether I wanted Alison to come up to my room or not. Then she came up the stairs, and it was too late.

Boy, if I hadn't been expecting her, I might not even have recognized her. Did she look cool! She had on a long black dress with diamond (or something) earrings. She had makeup all over her face—lipstick, red stuff on her cheeks, and black gunk all over her eyes. She looked about fifteen years old.

"Hey, you look neat," I said. "Come on in."

"Thank you," she said, in a sort of polite voice. She came in the door and stood there. I stood there, too.

"Your room's very nice," Alison said, in the same polite way.

"Yeah," I said. "It's big."

"It sure is," she said. "It's really big."

We stood there some more.

"Well, listen," I said, "let's get going. Want me to sit down so you can draw the mustache?"

"Okay, sit here." She pulled out my desk chair. I sat down and gave her the pencil. She began to draw. It tickled my nose.

"Hold still!" Alison said. She sounded more like herself.

"Okay," I said, "but don't push so hard. It feels funny."

"It *looks* funny," said Alison, giggling. "You should see yourself, Stuart. You look like a movie star or something."

"Let me see," I said. I went across the room to my chest where I have a mirror and looked. Wow! You would be surprised what a big difference a mustache makes on a person. I looked funny, but in a way I looked kind of cool, too. I wiggled my face around in the mirror. It looked pretty good. Maybe I'll have a mustache when I grow up.

I turned around. "Let's go."

Alison was bent over my desk. When I said that, she suddenly straightened up and stepped back. I wondered what was wrong.

Then I realized. Oh, no! She must have seen my pen pal letter, the one that I never got around to mailing. Damn! I should have just mailed it, instead of waiting to change it. Oh, man! I wonder if she read the whole stupid letter.

"Ready?" Alison said, sort of weakly.

I decided to pretend that I hadn't noticed anything.

"Okay," I said. "Let's go."

I guess Alison was going to pretend the same thing. "That's a nice banner, Stuart," she said. She was back to that polite voice again.

"Thanks," I said.

Just when I was trying to act so cool, I had spoiled it all because of that dumb letter.

I turned off the light, and we went downstairs.

Mom came into the hall. I hoped she wasn't going to say something embarrassing. That would be the last straw.

She did. "Well, you're a good-looking couple," she said.

"So long," I said. I wanted to get out fast.

"Don't be late," Mom said.

"I have to be back by ten," Alison said.

"Oh, that's fine, then," said Mom.

It was really dark out. "Where do you want to go first?" I asked.

"Let's go to some block where nobody knows us," Alison said. That sounded good. I felt better outside. It was nice, walking along in the dark with pumpkin faces in people's houses and other kids rushing along the street, yelling. It wasn't even scary, the way it used to be when we were little. I stopped to pick up a stick.

"Look, Alison," I said. I put the stick in my mouth and pretended to smoke it like a cigar. She laughed.

We were walking toward School Street. There were a lot of kids on the corner. They said "Hi" when we came up. When we walked away, I heard them arguing about who we were. I guess we looked mysterious to them.

We went up to the first house on the street. There was a jack-o'-lantern in the window. We rang, and a little kid about Jimmy's age came to the door. He held out a basket of Tootsie Rolls. He didn't say anything.

"Who is it, Herbie?" somebody called.

"A man and a lady," he called back.

Alison and I looked at each other and tried not to laugh. Then we grabbed a couple of Tootsie Rolls each and said thanks and ran down the sidewalk, breaking up.

"A man and a lady!" Alison yelled.

"We really fooled him!" I said.

"I guess we do look pretty sophisticated."

"I guess so," I said. "It's probably pretty hard for a little kid to tell, the way we look."

"Yeah," Alison said. I wondered if she'd forgotten the letter by now.

At the next house, a lady came to the door. "Oh, are you a tramp?" she asked me. Then she turned to Alison. "I can see you're a glamorous movie star."

Alison held out her skirt and bowed. "Oh, yes," she said. "Out here in Hollywood, everybody is glamorous."

The lady laughed and gave us popcorn balls.

The next house was dark.

"Do you suppose they're not home?" I asked.

"Let's go see anyway," Alison said.

I didn't like the idea of walking up those dark steps much, but I didn't want to say so. So we went up, and I looked through the little glass window in the door. Suddenly it opened.

"Whoooooo!" someone yelled, and a skeleton jumped out at us. Somebody must have been hiding there, waiting.

"Aah!" screamed Alison, running back down the steps.

I ran after her. On the porch, the skeleton laughed and a light went on inside.

"Scared ya," somebody called.

"Oh no, you didn't," I called back. But I felt sort of jumpy.

"He really scared *me!*" Alison laughed. "Oh, wow, am I glad I'm with you, Stuart! I wouldn't want to be out alone on a night like this." She pulled her shawl around her.

Now I felt a whole lot better. This was fun. I decided to test whether Alison had read my letter or not. Maybe she hadn't. We were walking past an empty lot, with no house to go to.

"I'm going to write to this friend in Michigan about the skeleton," I said. "I write him a lot of crazy letters. He'll think the skeleton was funny."

"Did Peter really live next to the Empire State Building?" Alison asked right away.

Oh, wow! That meant she really had read my dumb letter.

"Not exactly," I said. "I just write stuff like that sometimes, to make my letters more interesting."

"Oh," Alison said. We walked on. "Well, anyway," she said, "it's just a letter. How would *he* know whether you're making things up or not?"

"Yeah," I said. "Besides, that was an old letter. I wasn't even going to send it." I was glad I could explain that much to her.

We were in front of a house with lights on all over. When we rang the bell, a lot of people yelled inside. Some high-school kid answered the door. She was dressed up like a hippie.

"Hi," she said. "Come on in."

The living room was full of kids. They had really loud music playing, and some of them were dancing.

"Come on in and get some snacks," the girl said, leading us into the dining room.

I felt out of place because they were all much older than us. But I figured they wouldn't be able to tell how old we were. The way we looked, nobody could tell.

"Want some cider?" the girl asked.

She poured us cider and passed us a plate of doughnuts. We sat down at the dining-room table and watched the kids dancing in the living room. They didn't have fancy costumes, just some masks and beads and old clothes, like us. It was a neat party. I'd never been to a party like this one before.

"Wanna dance?" the girl asked. "Go ahead."

I don't really know how to dance. Not much, anyway.

Alison said, "I guess we better be going, thanks."

"Well, take another doughnut," the girl said. She looked at us. "Do I know you?" she asked.

"I don't think so," I said. "I'm Stu. She's Alison. We live on Seneca."

"Well, I guess I don't," the girl said. "It's hard to tell, on a night like this. You look like some tenth graders I know."

When Alison and I got out of there, we broke up again.

"Wow!" I said. "Wait till I tell Peter about this. Everybody thinks we're so *old!*"

Alison laughed. "We sure fooled them," she said. Then she sort of jumped. "Hey," she said, "we better go home. It must be getting late."

I didn't want to quit yet. "What time is it?" I asked.

"I don't know. I don't have a watch."

"Neither do I," I said. Then I had an idea. "Listen, let's sneak up on somebody's porch and look inside for a clock."

"Hey, yeah!" said Alison. "Be really quiet, though, okay? We don't want them to catch us."

We went up the steps of the next house as quietly as we could. There were lights on, but nobody came to the door. I tiptoed across the porch and looked in the living-room window. The TV was on, but no one was there. I couldn't see any clock. I looked over the mantel and on a table, but there wasn't one. I tried to see into the kitchen, in case there was a clock in there. All of a sudden, a lady came downstairs. I grabbed Alison and pulled her back. "Let's get out of here!"

We ran down the steps as fast as we could and stood on the sidewalk, laughing.

"Wanna try one more place?" I asked.

"Sure," Alison said.

This time we sneaked around to the back of the house. There was a kitchen window, but it was too high to see in.

"Here," Alison whispered. She put a log from the people's woodpile under the window. I stood on it, but I still wasn't high enough to see in.

"Try one more," I whispered.

Alison brought another log, and I put it on top of the first one. It made a wobbly kind of step, but I got up on it. Now I could see inside. A man and woman were sitting at the kitchen table, drinking coffee. I looked for a clock. Then the log slipped and thumped against the wall.

The man looked up at me. He jumped from his chair.

"Run!" I yelled to Alison. "Run!"

We grabbed each other and ran down the driveway as fast as we could. The back door opened and someone called, "Who's there?" But by that time Alison and I were way across the street. We kept running till we were safe. Then we stopped to catch our breath. We were still laughing.

"We're crazy!" I said. "If we want to find out what time it is, we can just go to somebody's door and ask them."

"But this is more fun," Alison said, panting. "Listen," she said, "let's go back to my house. We can sneak up and look in *my* kitchen window and see the clock. If it isn't ten, we can stay out longer."

So we did that, walking pretty fast the last couple of blocks in case we were late. There was nobody out anymore on our street. We got to Alison's driveway and turned in. I bumped right into something.

"Ow!" I said.

"Be quiet," giggled Alison. "What happened?"

Whatever it was, it moved. "It's Jimmy's tricycle," I said.

"Well, look out," said Alison. "Push it over on the grass so my dad doesn't run into it in the morning."

When I pushed the tricycle, I bumped it into a tree and the bell rang.

"Be quiet!" Alison said. "Don't let them hear us yet."

She tiptoed over to her kitchen window, looked in, and came back.

"It's about two minutes of ten," she said. "Man, is it lucky we came back now!"

"Yeah," I said. "Well, I guess you better go in."

"Yeah," said Alison. "I guess I better." She stood there and I stood there. Then Alison reached out and bopped me on the shoulder.

"So long, Stuart," she said. "I had a good time."

Then she started up her steps. "Me, too," I yelled after her. "See ya tomorrow."

I watched Mrs. Henning open the door and Alison go in. Then I walked home.

"Have a good time?" Mom asked when I went in.

"Yeah," I said. "It was fun."

"Go far?" Dad asked.

"Not too," I said.

"That Alison's such a sweet girl," Mom said.

"She's okay," I said. "Well, good night."

They both said good night.

That was my best Halloween so far. Even if Alison saw my letter and everything. It seems like a long time since I wrote that letter. A lot of things have happened. I still can't figure out how come I never noticed about Alison before. I guess you even have to practice noticing.

8

Alison got her backboard that Saturday, and on Monday I went over to check it out. It was up on the garage. I pretended I had a ball and dribbled up her driveway toward it, pivoted, and jumped up, just to get the feel of it. Just then Alison came out.

"Want to see the ball?" she asked.

"Sure," I said.

Alison got the ball out of the garage. It was a beauty. It even smelled new. I bounced it a couple of times to test it out, and then I jumped up and sank one in. Neat-o! I caught the rebound and shot again, but I missed. Alison and I both chased after the ball. She grabbed it, pivoted, and shot. Perfect.

"Nice one," I said. I caught her rebound and dribbled toward the basket for the lay-up. The ball sank right in. I love to watch a ball drop through the net like that.

Alison caught the ball and brushed some leafy stuff off it.

"Where'd you get it?" I asked her.

"Paramount Sports," she said. "Dad bought the most expensive backboard they had. The ball was second most. Dad said the backboard had to be good so it would last till Jimmy's in high school."

"Was Jimmy excited?"

"Sure, I guess so. He went with us, and all the salesmen said 'Hi, fella' and stuff like that. People always think he's cute. Dad made him try holding different balls, but he dropped them."

"Does your dad think he can teach Jimmy now?"

"Not right now," Alison said. "He thinks that having the backboard up will give Jimmy the urge to learn."

"Is that some kind of psychology?" I asked.

"I guess so," Alison said.

It seems to me it would be better psychology for Jimmy to want to be like Alison. I bet that will happen. Especially if Alison gets to take basketball in gym with us. Coach Schultz hadn't said anything about it yet, and I didn't want to tell Alison, in case Mom was wrong.

Jimmy came out. "Hi, Stuart," he said. "We have a new backboard!"

He always tells you what you already know.

Jimmy pulled the ball away from Alison. Then he squatted way down, jumped up, and pushed the ball out with both hands. When it came down, he ran after it. The ball rolled along the driveway and onto the lawn. Jimmy stumbled along after it. When he caught up with it, he fell down on it and lay there, laughing.

"It's going to be a while before he makes the Knicks," I said to Alison.

"Yep," she said. "First, it's going to be you and me."

"Hey, wouldn't it be funny if two basketball stars came from the same block in the same town?" I said.

"It would be neat," said Alison. "Listen, you're supposed to come in. Mom saw you. She made chocolate chip cookies."

"Coming in, Jimmy?" I asked.

"I'm gonna ride around," Jimmy said. He pulled his tricycle out of the garage. If they had tricycle teams, Jimmy would be a star right now.

Mrs. Henning smiled at me when we went in. She always used to hug me when I came over, but she doesn't do that anymore. I wouldn't mind that much, but I guess she thinks I would.

She poured glasses of milk for us. Then she picked some cookies off the rack with the turner and put them on a plate.

"They ought to cool off for a minute more," she said, "but I don't suppose you want to wait. Look out for the chocolate chips, now. Don't burn your tongues."

The cookies were delicious. Mrs. Henning is like mothers on TV shows, always baking things. Mom doesn't even *buy* cookies, unless we're having company.

"Take another one, Stuart," Mrs. Henning urged. "I made plenty."

I had already had four, but I always eat a little more than I think I want to at the Hennings'. I took one more.

"Want to play one-on-one after school this week?" Alison asked.

"Sure, unless Peter comes over," I said.

"Who's Peter?" asked Mrs. Henning.

I was sorry I brought it up. I didn't want to get into it right now. "He's this new kid in our class," I said.

"I didn't know you had a new boy in school, Alison," Mrs. Henning said. "That's good. It's good to make new friends."

"Yeah," Alison said. She looked at me, and I knew what she was thinking.

There was a honk in the driveway. "Well!" said Mrs. Henning. "Raymond's home early." She began to clear up the baking things. Alison jumped up and took our milk glasses to the sink.

I wished I had gone home before Mr. Henning came, but now I was stuck. Pretty soon we heard him talking outside with Jimmy. "I want to ride some more!" Jimmy was yelling.

Mr. Henning pushed the door open. "Come in and talk to your daddy, big boy," he said, pulling Jimmy into the kitchen by his sleeve.

"I want to go out!" said Jimmy.

"Now, you stay inside like Daddy wants you to," said Mrs. Henning. "I'll give you a nice hot bath, and then you can have your supper."

"That's right," said Mr. Henning. "Hello, Thelma. Hi, doll. Hey there, Stuart." He pushed my shoulder. "See our backboard out there?"

"It's neat," I said. "I like it a lot."

"Yeah, well, in a few years we're gonna make a basketball star out of this guy," Mr. Henning said, looking at Jimmy. "All it takes is the will to win, right, Stuart?"

"Yeah, I guess so," I said.

"No guess about it," said Mr. Henning. "That's what it takes: practice and the will to win."

"*I* practiced today, Dad," Alison said.

"Sure, doll, good for you," said Mr. Henning. "Just don't wear yourself out. Remember, you're not as tough as those big fellas."

Alison didn't say anything. Mr. Henning took off his coat and set down his case. He sells business supplies. Mrs. Henning picked up the coat and the case and took them into the hall.

"Wait till you hear what I heard today," Mr. Henning called after her.

"What?" Mrs. Henning came back.

"Feder, down at Feder's Hardware, told me," said Mr. Henning. "He says he was waiting on this fella Saturday, the guy was buying fifteen dollars of this, twenty dollars of that, said he was fixing things up in his new place on Woodburn Road. Feder says some colored woman walks in and comes up to this guy and puts her arm around him, and the guy says, 'Anything else you need, honey?' And she says, 'Maybe some curtain rods.' The guy says, 'Sure,' and they buy enough hardware for six picture windows. How about that? I'd sure like to see that guy's face if his wife walked in and caught him buying curtain rods for some colored woman. I don't know how a man thinks he can get away with hanky-panky like that. Feder said they walked out together laughing and hugging, big as you please."

"It's too bad for a married man to carry on that way in public," Mrs. Henning said. "And on a Saturday, too."

Alison looked at me. I had to say something.

"He wasn't carrying on, Mr. Henning," I said. "I bet that man was Peter's father, and the woman was his wife. Peter's mother. I already met her. She's nice. Peter's the new boy in our class."

Mr. Henning looked at me like I was crazy.

"Are you telling me that we've got a man with a colored wife moving onto Woodburn Road?" he demanded.

"They've already moved," I said.

Mrs. Henning said, "Raymond, maybe we better find out the whole story before you start worrying."

"I don't know if I'm going to be able to *take* the

whole story," Mr. Henning said. He turned to me. "You say the kid's in your class?"

"One of them," I said. "Peter. His brother's in ninth grade. His sister's only three."

"Oh, my God," Mr. Henning said. He opened the refrigerator door and took out a can of beer. "Believe me, this is just the tip of the iceberg. You watch," he said to Mrs. Henning. "By the time Jimmy goes to school, there'll be colored in every grade." He pulled the tab and took a long swallow of beer. "Not that I have anything against the colored," he said.

"Of course not," Mrs. Henning said nervously, picking up Mr. Henning's beer can tab and throwing it in the trash.

"But they're better off with their own kind, the same as we are," Mr. Henning said. "Intermixing, moving into a white neighborhood, that's not right."

Oh, man. It was awful to have him talk like that. I just wished he could *see* Peter's family. How could he say that if he saw them?

"Take my advice, Stuart." Mr. Henning looked at me. "Don't you get mixed up in any of this. Stay away. Don't bother them, and they won't bother you. That's the best way to handle it."

I looked at Alison. She looked scared. I didn't know what to say. I wanted to explain to him, but how could I?

"Well, I guess I better go now," I said. "So long,

Alison. So long, Mrs. Henning. Thanks for the delicious cookies."

I ran all the way home. I felt awful. But I knew one thing. I wasn't going to let Mr. Henning tell me what friends to have.

9

The next Thursday, the first day Peter didn't have to go to the dentist, he came over to my house. He walked home with Alison and me. It was fun walking along, the three of us. Peter told us about his teacher last year. She made the whole class memorize a poem called "Trees" because the man who wrote it had lived near their town. One kid in Peter's class made up a parody, a dog's-eye view of trees.

> *I think that I shall never pee*
> *On something lovely as a tree.*

The teacher saw it, and before she could stop herself, she laughed. So then she had the class make a collection of all the parodies they knew, only with no dirty words allowed. Peter knew a lot of them. Alison and I already knew some of the ones he told us. We walked along singing, "On top of spaghetti, all covered with cheese, I lost my poor meatball, when somebody sneezed." We laughed all the way home.

I wondered if Alison would feel left out when Peter and I went on. I didn't want to hurt her feelings, but just this once I wanted to be alone with Peter. Alison seemed to know that. She catches on to things before you have to go through a long explanation. When we got to her house, she said she had to help her mother shampoo the rugs, and she turned and started down her driveway.

"See ya tomorrow," she said.

"See ya," we said.

Jimmy ran out the back door and jumped at her, as hard as Rover jumps at me.

"That's her brother," I told Peter. "He rides his tricycle around like Evel Knievel."

"How old is he?" Peter asked.

"Three. His father already put up a backboard for him."

"How could a little kid like that shoot baskets?" Peter asked.

"That's the thing," I said. "He can't. But anyway, Alison can use it. She's really good."

"Is Alison your girlfriend?" Peter asked.

I was surprised he asked that, when I had just begun to figure it out myself.

"Yeah, I guess so," I said.

"I had a girlfriend in New Jersey," Peter said. "But I couldn't go over to her house."

"How come?"

"Her father didn't want her to go around with a black kid."

"You aren't black!" I said.

"Yes, I *am*," Peter said. "You better get that, Stuart."

"What I meant was, you don't *look* black," I explained. I hoped I hadn't hurt Peter's feelings.

"It's not just looks," Peter said. "It's how you feel, and who your ancestors are. I'm white from Dad's side and black from Mom's. I'm both, not just one thing the way most people are."

He sounded proud. He must have thought about it a lot.

Rover dashed up to us, flat out.

"Hey, is that your dog?" Peter asked.

"That's old Rover," I said. Rover shot past us and headed for the corner. He made a swinging U-turn and raced back, slamming to a stop against us. He jumped up on me, wiggling all over, and then he jumped onto Peter. He yipped and snuffled, and his tail went *thonk*.

I bent down and held him still. "Good old Rover," I said. "Yes, I'm glad to see you. This is Peter. He'll be your friend."

Rover flopped down on his back and bounced around with his legs in the air. Then he straightened up and began to walk ahead of us, calmly, toward the house.

"Man!" Peter laughed. "I never saw a dog act like that before. Is he crazy or something?"

"Nah," I said. "Just glad to see us."

"Does he do that every day?"

"Yep," I said. "That's his normal hello."

"You're lucky," Peter said. "We can't have a dog because of Diane. She's allergic."

Rover was waiting for us on the porch, wiggling all over. He snuffled at Peter while I took the key off the window ledge and opened the door. "Come on in," I said.

I got some apple juice and big bowls of the special granola my mother mixes up with raisins and nuts.

"It tastes like it has honey in it," Peter said.

"She puts that in, too," I said.

Peter asked me to get Mom to write down the ingredients. It turns out that he and Geoffrey like to cook. Peter knows how to make spaghetti.

"Mom said we might have to take home ec in junior high," I said. "And the girls take shop."

"Geoffrey took home ec two years ago," Peter said. "He even made a chocolate layer cake."

"Mom also said the girls might have basketball with us in gym from now on," I said. "They're trying to make everything equal in school."

"I might not like that so much," Peter said.

"How come?"

"Well, see, I'm not that good in basketball," Peter said. "I wouldn't especially want to shoot in front of a lot of girls."

I had never thought Peter would feel shy about anything.

Peter liked my room a lot. "You could practically have a backboard in here, it's so big," he said.

"I know it!" I said. "But I can't." I explained about my parents and the thumping. Peter and I tried to think of other things I could do with all the space. Maybe bowling, but that would make even more noise. Every good thing we thought of made noise.

We decided to shoot some baskets and then walk downtown. "I always go to the newsstand and read *Sports Illustrated*," I told Peter. "I usually only get to read about a page at a time, though. Mr. Stahlmier doesn't like you to hang around. He says, 'If you want to read it, buy it.'"

"I wish our house was closer to downtown," Peter said.

"Yeah, but you've got a pool," I said.

"Mom and Dad are draining it this weekend," Peter said. "They say it's too cold to swim anymore. I don't see why they have to drain it so soon. What if we got a heat wave or something?"

"Well, we probably won't," I said. "Not in Kansas in November."

"Yeah, but what *if*? There wouldn't be time to fill up the pool again."

"One thing about parents," I said, "is that they always want to finish things up. Like, they want to take down the Christmas tree as soon as New Year's is over."

"Yeah!" Peter said. "That's exactly how my

parents are. They start picking up the newspaper before you've even finished reading it."

"Yeah," I said. "They always want to put things away." It's funny how parents are all the same.

When we went out to shoot baskets, I could see that Peter really wasn't that good. He was fast, but he didn't have the technique.

I grabbed a rebound away from him and dropped a neat hook shot through the hoop.

"Man, I wish I could do that," Peter said.

"I could probably teach you," I told him.

"Yeah, but you have to have the talent to begin with," Peter said.

"I don't know." I never thought I had any talent for making friends, but look at me now. "You can do a lot with practice," I said. Maybe someday I'll tell Peter how I used to be, before he came.

We decided to go downtown. I took some money from my bank in the kitchen. If Mr. Stahlmier bugged me this time, I'd *buy* a magazine. That would show him.

Rover started to follow us. He knows he isn't allowed to go downtown, but he tries. He hunches way down on his stomach and slinks along behind you. If you turn around, he plays dead.

I said, "Stay, Rover," in my dog obedience school voice. Rover has never been to dog obedience school and neither have I, but I like to act as though we have, so people will think Rover is that kind of alert, well-trained dog.

Every step we took, Rover slinked along a little bit more. Nobody was looking, so I gave him a little push back with my foot. "Go home, you stupid dog," I said.

"He isn't stupid," said Peter.

"I know, but he's a real drag sometimes."

"I wouldn't think he was a drag if I had him."

That's what people who don't have a dog always think. You have to try something out yourself to know what it's really like. I could never know how it feels to be Peter, and he could never know what it's like to be me. But when you have a good friend, you can begin to understand.

At the next corner, Rover finally turned around and went home. Peter and I walked on downtown.

10

All the way downtown, Peter kept noticing things I never pay any attention to, because they were new to him.

"Look at that tree," he said in the next block. "That is some old tree. I bet it's about two hundred years old." He stretched his arms out against it. They hardly went halfway around.

I must have gone past that tree a million times, but I never thought about how old it was.

We walked on. When we got downtown, Peter wanted to look at the Veterans' Memorial. It's in a fenced-in park between Main Street and Tulsa Avenue. There's a statue of a Civil War soldier with a cannon and a pile of cannon balls in a pyramid next to it. I used to try to get one of the cannon balls loose when nobody was around, but they're cemented together.

The statue has the names of Civil War soldiers from Clayton on it. I guess that's the only war people ever expected to have, back then. Next to it there's a stone marker with the names of people who died in World War I and World War II. For Korea and Vietnam, there are just wood plaques. I know somebody on the Vietnam plaque: John Emery Holton—Buddy Holton. He used to be an usher at church. He passed the collection plates. Buddy died on the next to last day of the Vietnam War. That seems so unfair, when he had almost made it.

"I knew him," I told Peter, pointing to Buddy's name.

Then I noticed something funny. There were three big guys standing behind a parked car across the street, looking at us. All of a sudden I got scared. They looked strange. I got the feeling they were waiting for us. I wondered if they had some reason to be after us. One of them nodded to the others. The light changed. They started across the street, heading straight for us. One of them had on a plaid jacket, the others had black ones. Now I was sure. They were coming to get us!

"Hey, Peter!" I yelled.

Peter looked up and saw them. Right away, he jumped behind the statue. "Look out!" he called. "Get over here!"

The three guys came closer. They were talking to each other real loud, like they meant us to hear them.

"You wouldn't know it to look at him," one of them said.

"You can tell, though," said the one in the plaid jacket.

They jumped over the little fence and came right up to us.

One of them reached out and grabbed me by my sweater sleeve.

"Hey!" I yelled.

He pulled me up to him and put his face against mine. Then he spit. The spit stuck on my cheek. It felt thick and warm. He had blond hair and a thin, blond beard.

"Whattaya know," he said. "A nigger lover. That's what you are, right, punk? A nigger lover."

"Cut it out!" I said. I tried to pull back, but he had me by the arm. I looked in back of me for Peter.

The other two guys had pulled Peter away from the statue. I saw one of them push his knee into Peter's stomach and knock him down. The other guy rolled Peter over and twisted his arms behind his back.

"Ow!" Peter shouted. "What the hell do you think you're doing!"

"Shut up," said the guy who had pushed him down. He twisted Peter's arms harder. Peter was digging his feet into the ground, trying to push his body up.

I gathered all my strength and pulled away from the guy who was holding me. Then I ran over to Peter and punched the guy holding Peter's arms. I punched his stomach so hard it hurt my hand. He grunted. I felt him let go some.

"Hey, look out, you crazy kid!" the guy yelled. I looked around. The other two were in back of me. They must have been about six feet tall, and really mean looking. They moved toward me and then one of them punched me in the back so hard I fell down. My ear hit the sharp edge of the statue. It felt like it had been ripped right off. I felt sick. The punch hurt my back, all the way through to my stomach. I tried to push up, but one of the guys put his foot on my neck. I could still turn my head, but all I saw was the dirt.

Peter was yelling. I tried to yell too. I must have shouted "Help!" about twenty times while I lay there. But I couldn't yell very loud. It hurt every time I tried.

"This town don't want people like you," one of the guys said to Peter in a low voice. "You *or* your brother."

"Or his friend," said the guy with his foot on my neck. When he said that, I reached up and twisted his foot, hard. He lost his balance and fell down on his stomach. I jumped on him and pounded his back with my fists. The guy twisted around, threw me off, and held me down. "Listen, you better look out, you little punk. I could *really* hurt you."

Then he kicked me in the side. I thought the pain would kill me. My ear felt like it was on fire.

I didn't think I could take any more, but I figured that it couldn't get much worse, so I pushed up with all the strength I had left and rolled over onto my knees. The guy who was kicking me started to push me down, but I dodged him. I stood up as much I could and tried to get over to Peter.

Just then Peter got up on his knees. "Run!" he shouted at me. "Stu! Run!"

I turned and tried to run, stumbling across the little park toward the fence. Maybe I could reach the street and get help.

Just then, car brakes screeched, and a man jumped out of his car and ran toward me.

"Hey, you!" he yelled at the guys. I looked back and saw two of them jump away from Peter. Then they all took off and ran in the other direction. The man chased after them, but then he stopped and turned back, just as Peter came limping over to me.

The man grabbed us both in his arms. "What's happening?" he asked. "Are you all right?" He held us steady. I could feel my heart thumping.

"Those hoodlums!" he said. "I couldn't believe what I was seeing!"

He wiped my ear with a handkerchief. It hurt. The handkerchief was all bloody. There was blood on the front of my sweater and on my jeans. Oh, man, there was even blood on my good Adidas! Damn them!

The man brushed Peter off. Peter had a bloody

cut on one arm and a bruise on his forehead. He was holding his hurt arm with the other hand. His jacket sleeve was torn, and his pants were ripped down the side.

"Just let me get my hands on those guys," he said.

Then the man said, "I better drive you home so somebody can call a doctor. Where do you live?"

"You could just take us both to 125 Seneca Street," I told him.

"Hoodlums!" the man said again.

He helped us into the back seat of his car and started up. "Now then," he said. "What happened? How did it start?"

I couldn't figure it out. "They were just standing there, like they were waiting for us," I said.

"They were probably those guys from Geoff's school," Peter said. "It's just what Geoff said might happen, only they saw me first."

"How would they know you?" I asked.

"Geoff said they'd been hanging around our block," Peter said. "They found out what we look like. And when they saw me coming downtown, that was their chance. I'm smaller than Geoffrey." He sat back against the car seat. He looked beat.

"But why would they want to go after kids like you?" the man asked.

"See, my mother's black," Peter said. "My dad's white. We just moved here." Then he sort of bent over and choked.

I put my hand on Peter's arm. "Peter," I said. "Listen, Peter, they're just jerks. They don't know anything."

"Yeah," Peter said. He leaned over farther. He looked like he was going to throw up.

The man honked angrily at a car that was going slow in front of us. "I don't care *what* color your mother or father are," he said. "We can't have teenagers beating up children in the middle of Clayton. Those hoodlums!" he said again.

"I hate them," Peter said through his teeth.

"Me too." My ear had started to throb and the ache in my stomach was stronger. "Did you get hurt bad?"

"I think I'm okay," he said. "It's mostly my arm. What about you?"

"My stomach and my ear. I've never been beaten up before. It's horrible."

"It happened to me once before," Peter said. "I got a nosebleed that time."

"How'd you get away?" I asked.

"I ran!" Peter said. "It was only one guy."

"In a way," I said, "we did pretty good, two against three, and them so much bigger."

"Yeah," Peter said. "You really fought hard, Stuart. Thanks."

"That's okay," I said. "I'm glad I was there." And that was true.

The man turned onto Seneca Street and slowed down to look for our house.

"It's the one across the street with the dog in front," I said. Rover's ears went up when we got close. He started to run around the house, but then he suddenly stopped and came back and stood there watching us. I wondered if he could tell that something was wrong. I waved at him through the car window. When the man helped us out, Rover didn't even jump up on us. He just followed us slowly as we walked up to the door.

Mom ran out. The man talked to her a minute, and then he said, "So long, fellas." We thanked him for the ride.

Mom made us lie down at each end of the couch. She washed off the bloody places and brought us blankets and drinks of water. Then she called Peter's house. Rover came in and licked us both. I put my hand into his soft fur.

"I wish my mom didn't have to find out," Peter said.

"It's no fair!" I said. "Why should those guys be like that?"

"Yeah," Peter said.

Peter's father and mother came to get him. That was the first time they met Mom. I wished they didn't have to meet for such a reason. They talked in the hall for a second, and then they came in. Peter's mom bent over and kissed him. Her face was stiff.

"Oh, hon, how *could* they!" she said. "Does it hurt a lot?"

"It's not bad, Mom," Peter said. "It's okay."

Then she turned to me. "How are you, Stuart? I'm so sorry you got mixed up in all this."

"That's okay," I said. "I have to, because Peter and I are friends."

Peter's mom said, "Well, hon, I'm afraid you've found out what that means. The hard way." She looked sad.

I didn't want Mrs. Baker to think everything was terrible. "It's good you moved here!" I said. "Everybody in our class likes Peter!"

"I'm glad we came," Peter said, pulling himself up higher. "I like it here. Except for those dirty guys. I hate those guys."

Peter's dad was sitting on the arm of the couch, with his hand on Peter's shoulder. He looked very angry.

He said, "Don't waste your energy hating 'those guys.' They aren't going to bother you again. They've made their point. They've defended their turf against two little kids to show how tough they are. That's all they wanted."

"That better be all!" Peter's mother said. "The next time, we'll get the police after them. I'm not going to take any more of this."

"No," Mr. Baker said. "We won't have any more of this. We'll see that every school principal hears about it. I can't have my kids subjected to physical threats."

I heard Dad's car in the driveway.

"Oh, there's Mark," Mom said. "He'll be so glad to meet you." Then she stopped. "I never dreamed we'd all meet this way. . . ."

She went out to meet Dad in the kitchen. I heard Dad say, "What!" and Mom say, "Take it easy, Mark."

Then Dad came in. "How are you, Stu?" he asked me. He looked pretty upset.

"I'm okay, Dad," I said.

"And this is Peter," Dad said, looking down at him. "I've heard a lot of good things about you. Are you okay, Peter?"

"It's just my arm," Peter said.

Then Dad shook hands with Mr. and Mrs. Baker. He stood there holding their hands and looking at them. "I'm very glad to know you," he said. "I hope you won't hold this against Clayton. So many people will welcome you."

"Our neighbors already have," Mrs. Baker said. "And yesterday the Methodist minister came by. We're planning to join that church."

"That's *our* church," Mom said. "I'm glad."

"Hey, neat," I said to Peter.

Peter and I rested on the couch while our parents called the doctor. They called the *Tribune,* too.

"I want people to hear about this," Dad said. "We'll tell the facts before a lot of rumors get started."

I wondered what Mr. Henning would think when he heard the facts. I hoped he'd be sorry for what he said.

By the time we went to the doctor's to get checked out, I could tell that my parents and Peter's parents would be friends. It turned out that nothing was really wrong with me or Peter, except cuts and aches. The doctor put stuff that really stung on my ear and wrapped a bandage around my head. He made a sling for Peter's arm because he had a bad sprain.

I didn't get to bed till about eleven o'clock. Mom and Dad came up to say good night, the way they used to when I was little.

Dad pulled up my covers. "You've had a tough day. But you really came through."

Mom kissed me. "You're a good kid, Stuart," she said. "You make us awfully proud."

It felt wonderful to lie flat on my soft bed. My ear hurt, and my stomach ached, and my heart still thumped so I could hear it. But even so, I felt good. It was as if I had passed some kind of test, the way the young Indians did to prove they were worthy of the tribe. I never knew what I could take before. Now I know I can take a whole lot worse than I ever thought I could, if I have to. Maybe I'll have to, to stick with Peter. But we'll be okay. We're more than just friends now. We're like blood brothers.

11

Alison came over the next morning while I was eating breakfast.

"I came to see how Stuart is," she told Mom. Then she came in the kitchen. "Oh, your ear!" she said when she saw me. "Does it hurt?"

"It's okay," I said. "How did you hear about it?"

"We saw it in the *Tribune*," Alison said. "Here's yours." She gave Mom the paper.

"It's so *unfair*!" Alison said. "Three of them, and bigger than you. And why they did it is disgusting. Boy, if I'd been there I would have gone after them." She clenched her fists. "But I would have been scared," she added, with a little laugh.

"I was scared," I said.

"Well, I think you're real brave," said Alison. She sure knows how to make you feel good.

"Here it is," said Mom, putting the paper on the table.

It was just a little article on the back page. It gave Peter's and my name and said that we were attacked by three youths, names unknown. "Youths" is a pretty polite name for them, if you ask me. It said "alleged racial insults" were involved.

"Doesn't 'alleged' mean 'supposed to be'?" I asked Mom.

"That's right," she said.

"Well, those weren't any 'alleged' insults," I said. "They were real!"

"Of course they were," Mom said. "The paper's being careful. But they got the facts straight. A lot of people are going to be angry when they read this."

"Mom was," Alison said. "She thought it was terrible. She told me to tell you she hopes you're okay."

"Did your dad hear about it?" I asked Alison.

"No, he went to work before the paper came."

I wondered what he'd say when he found out. I knew one thing, though. I didn't care *what* he said.

At school, everybody acted like we were heroes. I sort of wished I had a sling like Peter's. It was more dignified. My bandage made me look like Mickey Mouse. But nobody laughed.

"Were you scared, Wilson?" Chip asked me.

"Sure," I said.

Robert said, "I guess you really showed *them*." Then he said, "You still going to practice basketball, with your bandage?"

"Sure," I said. "How come?"

"I just wondered," he said. He looked at me sort of funny. It seemed like he was waiting for me to say something.

I guessed what it was. "Wanna come over some afternoon?" I asked.

"Yeah, sure, if I can," he said. "I don't know if I can, though." He stopped. Then he said, "See, my mother makes me do all this stuff in the afternoons."

That was why he didn't come over before. I wonder why he never said so. Maybe he was shy. Hey, I never thought about that!

"Listen, Robert," I said, "any time you can come over, come. You can practice with me and Alison, and maybe Peter, if he doesn't have to go to the dentist."

"Thanks, Stu," Robert said.

"Sure," I said.

Then Annie pulled me over to the side of the room. "Is Peter's mother really black?" she asked.

I sort of tightened up. "Yeah," I said. "What of it?"

"Nothing," Annie said. "It's interesting, that's all. I just finished this book about a white boy who falls in love with a black girl, but in the end they break up. I wanted them to get married. I don't see why they shouldn't, if they really love each other."

"That's what I think," I said.

We were supposed to have assembly practice that day, but Miss Hansen called a class discussion instead. She asked Peter and me to tell about the fight.

"But why would they *do* that?" Annie asked, after we'd told everything that had happened.

"Because they're jerks!" Chip said.

"Because they never met anybody different before," said Robert.

"That's a good reason," Miss Hansen said right away. You could tell she liked Robert's answer better than Chip's.

"Well, that could change," I said. "Like, if other black families came to live in Clayton, so it was more ordinary to see them around."

"And if their kids went to school," Robert said, "then other kids would get to know them the way we know Peter."

"Yeah, and when you start to know somebody, then even if you're prejudiced, it would help you change your mind," Annie added.

"It's hard for some people to change their minds, though," Alison said. She was probably thinking about her father.

"It's not easy," Miss Hansen said. "But it's true that people who live in the same neighborhood or go to school together aren't so likely to worry about each other's differences."

The door opened, and Coach Schultz came in. He looked around. "Am I interrupting?"

"That's all right," Miss Hansen said. "We're not about to finish this discussion today. Go ahead."

"I have a couple of announcements," Coach Schultz said. "First of all: From now on, boys and girls are going to have most gym periods together. In the fifth and sixth grades, that means fitness activities and gymnastics and team sports like basketball will be together."

I knew it!

Alison shouted, "All right!"

A couple guys in back yelled, "Boo!"

"The girls don't know how to play basketball," Chip said.

"Oh, yeah?" Valerie poked him. "Wait and see!"

"I've heard some pretty good things about these girls," Coach said.

"Right," said Miss Hansen. "We have some real pros in this bunch."

Peter wasn't saying anything. I bet he didn't like the idea of playing in front of the girls. Well, he'll have to get used to it.

Coach said, "Another announcement: We're going to have an interschool basketball league this winter. All three elementary schools will have a team. I expect some of you will want to try out for it. Everyone here is welcome."

Alison grinned at me and stuck her thumb up.

———————

That afternoon Alison and I were practicing passes when Jimmy came out.

"Hey, Stuart, you have a bandage on," he said.

"Yeah," I said. "Here it comes, Alison."

She caught my pass, ran up to the hoop, and made a neat basket. I caught the rebound and put another one in.

"Coach Schultz should see us now," I said.

"He'll see," Alison said. "Just wait till tryouts."

We kept on practicing, dodging around Jimmy on his tricycle. We were really hot. Then I made a long shot from the grass behind the house.

"Oh, man," I said. "That one really hurt my stomach."

"We better sit down awhile," Alison said.

We sat on the steps and watched Jimmy ride around.

"I'm riding in a circle," he called.

Alison and I laughed. "It's a good thing he told us," I said. "I might not have noticed."

Mrs. Henning came to the door. "Oh, hello, Stuart," she said. "How are you?"

"I'm okay, thanks," I said.

"That was a terrible thing those teenagers did to you," she said. "Would you like a cookie?"

"Sure," I said.

Mrs. Henning went in and came back out with a big plate of raisin cookies. She called to Jimmy,

"Time to come in, Jimmy. Your father's going to be home any minute."

"One more ride around," Jimmy said.

I thought about going before Mr. Henning got there. But I decided not to. I wanted him to see what had happened to me. I wanted him to take back what he had said about Peter's family.

"Dad's going to say 'I told you so,' " Alison said.

"I know it," I said. "But I think I'll stick around anyway."

We watched the cars go past in front of her house. Then one of them slowed down and turned in.

"There he is," Alison said.

Mr. Henning drove up to us. Then he turned off the engine, rolled down his window, and leaned out.

"Hey there, Stuart," he said. "I hear you got into quite a fight. What did I tell you?"

"Yeah," I said. "They tried to beat us up. Three against two."

"What did I tell you?" Mr. Henning said again. "Those people are nothing but trouble. You should have stayed away from that boy."

"I can't, Mr. Henning," I said, as calm as I could. "Peter's my best friend."

Mr. Henning looked surprised. I thought he was going to say something mean. Instead, he said, "Well, you sure stuck up for him, didn't you. Got yourself pretty beat up, I hear. What's the matter with that ear?"

"I cut it," I said. "I fell on the Civil War statue."

"I hear you put up a pretty good fight," Mr. Henning said. "Fella down at Feder's Hardware told me. Said he heard something going on, but he wasn't sure what it was at the time."

"He did?" I said. If Mr. Feder had any nerve, he would have come out and helped us.

"Yeah, Feder told me about it this morning," said Mr. Henning. "Told me about the family, too. It seems his son's in school with the older boy, what's his name?"

"Geoffrey," I said.

"That's it," said Mr. Henning. "Feder says this Geoffrey's a great football player. Used to play fullback on his team back East. Says he wouldn't be surprised if he turns the team around out of their losing streak. Some of those colored fellas can be pretty good athletes, I'll admit that."

You could tell Mr. Henning never saw Peter play basketball.

"Well, you did stick up for your buddy," Mr. Henning said again. He shook his head. "I never thought things like this would happen in Clayton."

I wasn't sure what things he meant, but I wasn't going to ask. I didn't think Mr. Henning would change his mind just because some guy pushed me into a statue or because Geoffrey was a good football player. That's not the *point*. But I figured I better not try to explain everything to him right then.

"Hey, Dad," Alison said. "Guess what? Our

school's going to have tryouts for a basketball team!"

"Oh, yeah?" Mr. Henning said, catching Jimmy's handlebars. "Hey there, fella, can't you say hello to your daddy?"

"I wanna ride!" Jimmy said. He pulled away and rode off.

"You're going to have a basketball team, eh?" Mr. Henning said. "I'm glad to hear it. Start them young, teach them how to win. That's the way to do it. Think you'll make the team, Stuart?"

"I hope so," I said. "Alison too."

"Alison!" said Mr. Henning. "What kind of a team *is* it, anyway?"

"Just a regular team, from our school," I said. "We're going to be in a league and play all the other grade schools."

"They're going to let *girls* on it?" Mr. Henning asked.

"If they're good enough," I said.

Mr. Henning shook his head. "Since when are there girls on boys' basketball teams?"

"Coach Schultz said that's how it's going to be from now on," Alison said.

"Next thing you know," said Mr. Henning, "you won't be able to tell one sex from the other, the way things are going." He started up the steps.

"Stuart and I practiced passes all afternoon," Alison said.

Mr. Henning stood there for a minute, getting used to the idea.

Then he said, "Well, you want to keep at it, every day. Remember, practice makes perfect."

He went inside.

Alison and I looked at each other. She shrugged.

"You never can tell," I said.

"Yeah," said Alison. "Maybe he'll come around completely, someday."

"Yeah," I said. "Maybe all he needs is practice."

12

A couple of weeks later, when I was looking for some paper to do my homework on, I came across that old letter I wrote my pen pal. I read it over. I could hardly believe I had written that letter. I sure had a lot of new things to tell Marty. I got out my yellow pad and began a new letter. I thought of a funny way to start:

> Dear Marty,
>
> I wrote you a letter a long time ago, but guess what? My dog ate it up!

I looked at that. It *was* funny, but it wasn't true. Why should I make up stuff when I had so many interesting things to write about? I started again:

> Dear Marty,
>
> I haven't written for a long time because I have been very busy. First of all, our

school got a basketball team and guess what? I'm on it! My girlfriend is on the team too. (I guess you didn't know I have a girlfriend. Well, I do. She is cool.)

Another thing happened to me. Me and my friend went downtown, and some big guys (three) jumped us and tried to beat us up, for no good reason. We punched them back enough to hurt them, and then we ran and got away. It was some fight! I cut my ear on a statue, and Peter (my friend) hurt his arm. They wrote about us in the newspaper. (I will put a copy of the article in this letter so you can read it.) Now some people act like we are heroes.

We have basketball practice three days a week, and the other days I usually do stuff with Peter or this kid named Robert or Alison (my girlfriend). So that's why I have been so busy.

How are you? Did your dog eat up any more sandwiches? (Ha, ha.) Please write me back.

Your friend,
Stu Wilson

P.S. If you ever come to Kansas, try to go through Clayton. Then you could visit me and meet my friends.

"Stuart," Mom called upstairs. "Did you finish your homework yet?"

"Almost," I called back. I guess some things will never change.

BETTY MILES is the author of many popular novels for young readers, among them *The Secret Life of the Underwear Champ* and *The Trouble with Thirteen*. She frequently visits schools around the country to talk about books with students, teachers, librarians, and parents. Ms. Miles lives with her husband in Tappan, New York. They are the parents of three grown children.

BETTY MILES

"is solid gold!"
—Publishers Weekly

The Secret Life of the Underwear Champ

Starring in television commercials sure isn't what it's cracked up to be, discovers 10-year-old Larry Pryor. The shooting schedule conflicts with his baseball practice, and he actually has to wear makeup on film! But the biggest problem is what Larry's supposed to be modeling. They can't really expect him to go on TV in his underwear . . . can they?

An IRA-CBC Children's Choice
A Child Study Association Children's
Book of the Year
A Georgia Children's Book Award Winner
A Mark Twain Award Winner

The Trouble with Thirteen

Best friends Annie and Rachel don't long for pierced ears, eye makeup, or boyfriends. Life at age 12 is absolutely perfect—just the way it is. But when Rachel announces she's moving away, major changes begin to pull them apart just when they need each other the most. And now Annie wonders, "Is staying 12 forever worth it if you have to do it all alone?"

**Bullseye Books published by
Alfred A. Knopf, Inc.**

BARBARA PARK

"is one of the funniest writers around!"
—*Booklist*

The Kid in the Red Jacket

It was bad enough that Howard's parents moved the family to a street called Chester Pewe, but now they want him to be nice to his tagalong neighbor, who happens to be a six-year-old girl. How do they expect him to make any *real* friends with her around? At this rate, he could spend the rest of his life known only by the color of his sportswear!

**A *Parents' Choice* "Gold" Award Winner
An IRA-CBC Children's Choice**

Skinnybones

For the smallest kid on the baseball team, Alex "Skinnybones" Frankovitch has sure got a major league talent for wisecracking. But even Alex knows that there are some messes you *can't* talk your way out of, especially when it's a contest of skills with T. J. Stoner, the Little League legend with a perfect pitching record. . . .

**Winner of children's book awards in five states:
Georgia, Texas, Minnesota, Indiana, and Utah**

**Bullseye Books published by
Alfred A. Knopf, Inc.**